Catherine
refracted

Catherine refracted

Pure Slush Vol. 7

Pure
Slush

Catherine refracted Pure Slush Vol. 7 is edited by Matt Potter
and originally published by Pure Slush, June 2013.

Second edition of this print book published October 2014.

All stories are copyright of the individual authors.

Cover: portrait by Georg Christoph Grooth of the Grand Duchess Ekaterina Alexeevna
(later Empress Catherine II of Russia / Catherine the Great) painted circa 1745, St. Petersburg, Russia.
The portrait is in the collection of the Hermitage Museum, St. Petersburg, Russia.

ISBN: 978-1-925101-78-2

You can find *Pure Slush* at http://pureslush.webs.com/

All queries re *Pure Slush* can be made
via email to edpureslush@live.com.au

Copies of all *Pure Slush* books and eBooks can be bought at
http://pureslush.webs.com/store.htm

stories by

Claudia Bierschenk

Sarah Collie

Gay Degani

Mira Desai

Desmond Fox

Gill Hoffs

Juliet Beckman Hubbell

Kim Conklin Hutchinson

L.S. Johnson

Joyce Juzwik

Robert Mangeot

Todd McKie

Matt Potter

Stephen V. Ramey

Dusty-Anne Rhodes

Anne Scott

Andrew Stancek

Susan Tepper

Christine Tolley

dedicated to

Megan Hills

whose advice led me here

M.P.

Contents

and then some

Preface

A large blown-up photo of yet another palace Catherine the Great lived in or built or both – and there were so many – shone out from the wall, gold against a dark blue sky ... or that's what I recall, now, almost a year later.

The National Museum of Scotland in Edinburgh mounted the exhibition 'Catherine the Great: An Enlightened Empress', in conjunction with the publication of Robert Massie's new biography *Catherine the Great: Portrait of a Woman*. And I was in Edinburgh in July 2012 for four days, seeing the sights and catching tourist buses and yes, it *was* odd for an Australian tourist to visit an exhibition in the Scottish capital on the life of a German-born empress of Russia ... but perhaps that's a reflection of the modern world.

And looking at yet another portrait, I thought, Catherine led such a varied life and did so many different and interesting things ... has anyone ever really done her justice? (And how could they?) And perhaps there's a story in that – or a number of them – and wouldn't that be even more interesting: the *real* Catherine as seen by those who pretend to have known her?

I did later read Massie's biography – I bought it a month later, in the English-language section of a Berlin bookshop, the only copy – and finished it four five six turgid months later.

I hope you take far less time to read this version of Catherine's life. And find it infinitely less turgid!

Matt Potter, editor, *Pure Slush*, June 2013

Catherine's Life

1729 – born Sophie Friederike Auguste von Anhalt-Zerbst-Dornburg in Stettin, Pomerania (now Szczecin, Poland), daughter of Christian August, Prince of Anhalt-Zerbst (then a Prussian general and Governor of Stettin) and Johanna Elisabeth of Holstein-Gottorp.

1739 – first meets her cousin, Peter of Holstein-Gottorp, prospective heir to his maternal aunt, the ruling Empress Elizabeth of Russia.

early 1744 – arrives in Russia as prospective bride of Peter of Holstein-Gottorp.

June 1744 – converts from Lutheranism to Russian Orthodoxy and takes the name Catherine (*Yekaterina* or *Ekaterina*).

August 1745 – marries Peter in St Petersburg.

January 1762 – Empress Elizabeth dies and Peter succeeds her as Peter III of Russia.

July 1762 – Catherine becomes Empress and Autocrat of All the Russias following a coup. Eight days later, Peter is killed.

November 1796 – Catherine dies, and is buried in Peter and Paul Cathedral in St Petersburg.

Other facts about Catherine

Catherine had court favourites, generals and diplomats among others, many of whom became her lovers. They included Sergei Saltykov, Grigory Grigoryevich Orlov, Stanislaw August Poniatowski (whom she later had crowned King of Poland), Alexander Vasilchikov, Grigory Alexandrovich Potemkin, Pyotr Zavadovsky and Prince Zubov.

Catherine had four children, three illegitimate: a daughter fathered by Stanislaw August Poniatowski, then another daughter and a son fathered by Grigory Grigoryevich Orlov. There is also some doubt as to the paternity of Catherine's eldest, her heir (later Paul I), either fathered by Peter III ... *or* by Sergei Saltykov.

Catherine's accomplishments are too too numerous and too too varied to mention here ... suffice to say that if an accomplishment is mentioned in this book, it's probably true.

aka Sophie

The Girl Who Loved Horses

by Sophie Friederike Auguste
von Anhalt-Zerbst-Dornburg, aged 13 ¾
and Claudia Bierschenk

Девушка, которая любила Кокей
(София Фредерике Августе ф.
-Анхальт- Церрст- Дорнбург,
13 ¾ лет)

Sophia Friederike

1) Давайте познакомимся
зовут меня Катрин
Я из самого скучного города
Об этом городе никто никогда
на ~~слышал~~ слышал

2) Свою мать ненавижу
Вот - сейчас сказала!
Она такая БЛЯДЬ
Это нецензурное
русское слово
Она по-русски не говорит

3) Ей хочется чтобы я
была бы выходит
замуж за Петра-
ему 12 лет!
Мой троюродный брат!
Он ужасно. Тьфу!
Он псих. Он

4) Всё это продолжает
таким образом
(если вам интересно)
для того что я стану
Королевой России!

5) Для того что ОНА моля
бы уехать отсюда!!
Она даже хочет
что я была бы
выходит замуж за свою БРАТА!

6) Представьте себе!
ужасно!

7) Однажды люди
говорят
"Она красота такая
такая популярная
женщина!
буду встречаться с
~~каким-либом~~
человеком →
красивым!

8) И люди говорят
в сто лет:
"Она была красивее
чем персиком
умнее чем мальчиком
жила в стеклянном
дворце
сделала Россию
французский
блеск

Блядь!

21

The Girl Who Loved Horses

adaptation into English from the Russian, by Desmond Fox

Let's be friends.
You can call me Catherine.
I come from the dullest place,
I bet you've never even heard of it.

I hate my mother. There, I said it.
She is such an old "blad".
That's Russian for a bad thing.
Mummy can't speak Russian.

She wants me to marry Peter.
He's my second cousin. He's 12.
And he is gross.
I wish he was dead.

All of this is going on,
if you want to know,
so that I marry him
and become Queen of Russia

so she can leave this dump.
She even wanted me
to marry her brother.
If you can believe it. Gross.

One day I will be queen.
And the people will all say,

"Isn't she pretty!
Isn't she popular!"
I will have any boy that I like. A pretty one.
And a hundred years from now they will say,

"She was pretty as a peach.
She was brighter than a boy.
She had a house that was made of glass.
She gave Russia the glamour of France."

Regent

by Mira Desai

Sophie traced her name in the frost-encrusted glass pane. Empress of Russia and all her domains ... Snow fell in large flurries covering the square in a blanket of white, and the dome of the Tsar's palace gleamed like a jewel in the distance. Sophie stepped back and watched her reflection in the glass pane. Picture perfect, each curl in place, the chin regal, the skin porcelain gleaming in the lamplight ... quite right for an Empress of the realm. For an Empress of the world really, whoever ruled Russia ruled the world, everyone knew that. Yet.

She quickly rubbed out the scrawl and whirled around to check, although there was no one in the room. Yet.

If only Mama hadn't gushed at the tea party at the Vasilyev's ... everything had gone wrong, starting with the shabby carriage they'd taken there and the seating — the most uncomfortable chair in a draft ... if only Mama hadn't felt the pinch at being provincial and genteel, her gown in last season's style. *Your majesty the Stettin Governor's wife*, with only her family connections, distant cousin to the sundry minor royals as armor, if only she'd held on to her tongue instead of working so hard to get even ... her daughter, in line to be the next Tsarina. The Empress herself favored her daughter, hadn't she specially called for them to visit so the young ones could make an acquaintance? The Empress thought she was pretty and fine-featured, the Empress would favor her bloodline over all others, she needed someone she could trust, didn't she? The ladies of the court had peered past their oriental fans and pince-nez and gently nudged her along with a comment here and a look there.

Word had reached the Empress before the tea had cooled in the samovars. Mama's carriage had left in a flurry an hour ago, yes, despite the driving snow.

Empress Sophie ... the words hung rich and gleaming. Hadn't she worked towards this? Deportment, language lessons, etiquette and yes, firearms ... she'd spent a lifetime learning about wars and loyalties and the price of serfs. Though that Peter wouldn't make much of a husband, even as a lad he'd been so spineless, gleefully cheering dogfights rather than going hunting, pale, sickly and prone to untruths, she knew he wouldn't be much of a husband ... and yet. Tsarina.

Just an hour ago, a chambermaid, a young girl from a village in her province in Prussia, had slipped her a crumpled note. The hunchback, the one with the beady eyes and evil manner, wanted an audience. The Count Lestocq spoke well of him, he wrote.

He'd slipped in without as much as a knock, as if he'd walked through walls. And he'd been direct.

"I know what you want. And that you'll never get it without my help. Changing destiny lines is excruciating work. To carve the crown upon your palm I shall have to call upon the dark powers. The earth shall tremble."

"But can it be done?" she'd quivered, her fingers digging an angry red into her palms, her heart thudding.

"You doubt my strength?" he'd shrilled.

"No ... but ..."

"A pint of your freshly-drawn blood for the first six months after you're married. A lock of your hair and bats wings and a lizard skeleton ... my word shall be final. But you can be Tsarina."

"After Mama's careless ways the Empress is so angry ..."

"You think this is child's play? Thunder will jolt the earth, this pristine show will turn muddy and flood the rivers. Many will pay with their lives. But it can be done."

"Perhaps I could have a word with the Count ..."

"No one is to know. And I lay first claim upon your newborn."

Transvestite Balls

by Sarah Collie

Bright skirts swirled in a dizzying kaleidoscope: coppery orange and vibrant blue, buttercup yellow and shimmering purple. Couples filled the dance floor, stepping and turning to the music as lamplight shone on thousands of glittering jewels. Laughter filled the air, eddying in waves of whispers and rumours, the air rich with heady perfumes and the scent of wine and dazzling colour.

Catherine could hear snatches of whispered gossip from her seat; the scandal of the Russian court was as much a part of these evenings as the dancing. A hush fell over the crowd as one of the unlucky victims of talk drew close and began again as soon as she moved away. Whispering lips repeating second-hand stories of her shameful behaviour, on the terraces with a lowly Sergeant. The voices fell silent again, as a handsome man approached Catherine.

Seated, Catherine smiled up at her next partner, nodding her head as he offered his hand, clasped it, following him out into the whirling mass of dancers.

He was a tall man, broad-shouldered and dark. But despite his size, the Lieutenant was light on his feet, and graceful. Catherine smiled. So often, after a night of dancing with men unaccustomed to their change in outfit and unable to see their feet, she rode home in her carriage nursing bruised toes because the men had crushed hers.

Stifling a giggle, she thought the Lieutenant's violet, off-the-shoulder gown was a brave choice, especially since he had so much dark chest hair. And the feel of hair as she clasped his arm … though the hair was soft, she was used to the caress of velvets or embroidered silks against her fingers. It was not unpleasant, she thought, just … different.

Ah, but she admired his effort! The Lieutenant wore his long beard neatly braided in two rows secured with tiny violet bows matching his gown. He moved a little too close and the fabric bunched between them. Used to the bulky skirts, Catherine stepped back to allow more room.

He smiled in gratitude. Catching the smile she had tried to hide, he winked at her. "If we must wear such outfits it makes sense to do it properly I thought. I had my sister help me choose, do you approve?"

"You look very fetching, better than many of the outfits others have chosen, Lieutenant," Catherine told him, glad to have such a relaxed dance partner for once.

Catherine found the sensation of tailored silk against her thighs instead of layers of frilled undergarments and voluminous skirts to be quite freeing. No being weighed down or worrying about catching her skirt. And her hair, usually curled and pinned tightly on top of her head in a powdered pile, now tied loosely at the nape of her neck, swung as she danced.

She glanced around the room. Many of the men wore grim, tight expressions, uneasy with the pressure of their corsets and the starch in their ruffles and the swirl of their skirts. And they were so complimentary when the women wore such costumes!

The Lieutenant lifted an arm and she twirled, scanning the crowd. A couple caught her eye. The woman wore a long jacket cut in beautiful scarlet silk and danced with Catherine's own fiancé Peter. His dress was a horrible green, his skin more sallow than usual against the mucous-coloured satin. The girl, like Catherine, wore no powder on her dark glossy hair, her youthful skin smooth and translucent under the twinkling lights. She glowed with life and vigour.

Peter, with dark shadows under his eyes and pockmarked cheeks and powdered hair looked more at home in a sick room than a ballroom.

The music ended and the partners bowed.

"Thank you," Catherine said to the Lieutenant as he escorted her back to her seat. "You dance so well."

"It was my honour to escort such a beautiful lady. If there is ever anything I can do for you then it would be my pleasure to put myself at your disposal."

He bowed again and disappeared into the crowd.

Catherine looked after him uncertain of quite what he had meant. He was serious, as he had spoken, looking deep into her eyes as though trying to convey something unspoken. She felt a slow flush creeping over her, and sank into her seat again, looking around to see where he had gone.

Monsieur Seivers bowed stiffly. His dress was old-fashioned and buttoned high and drew attention to his long, thin neck, while his face was red and shining with sweat.

Despite her reluctance, despite the thought of touching his skin, wet and clammy under the peach-coloured satin, Catherine smiled and accepted his hand. She had no desire to dance with the sweaty Frenchman but there was no way to decline without causing offense, and at least moving around the room she might catch a glimpse of the Lieutenant again.

"Are you enjoying your time with us, Monsieur?"

"Yes, it has been quite interesting so far, the architecture is very different from what I am used to. But the cold air of Russia comes as a shock after the warmth of the French sunshine, Mademoiselle."

"I haven't seen your country, will you tell me about it?"

"Oh, it is very beautiful," he began. And she smiled as she tuned her ear to the music and tuned his voice out. Happy at the chance to talk about his homeland he relaxed, chattering about the beauty of Paris and the finery of French fashions and the elegance of the French court. Only his stepping on her toes brought her back to his monologue, and she winced, knowing tomorrow would be spent lying in her bedroom with ice on her toes.

Catherine smiled, and Monsieur Seivers continued talking, looking at Catherine and not looking at the other dancers.

Suddenly he pulled up, unable to dance on, pulling away, his skirts caught. A woman behind had stepped on his hem. Frowning, he tugged impatiently at his skirt. The woman lost her footing, and flung her arms out as she tried to save herself from falling, toppling over and slapping Catherine on the side.

Catherine grabbed Monsieur Seivers to steady herself, but the twist of his body and the tangle of his skirts pulled him towards her and the three fell sprawling on the floor, a mess of peach satin and thrashing limbs and humiliation.

Catherine shook with laughter as she fought her way through the yards of Monsieur Seivers' skirt. The music stopped and shocked silence filled the ballroom. All eyes were watching them. Looking up as she crawled to her knees, Catherine's eyes met those of her bearded Lieutenant. He stood above her and once again, offered his hand. And once again, she took it.

... waiting ...

Catherine's First

by Stephen V. Ramey

"I know your secret," Sergei Saltykov said.

You do? I thought. There was a reason that Empress Elizabeth's masquerades so often involved dressing as the opposite sex. Still, I was nearly certain that Sergei had not stumbled onto anything compromising. Handsome, he was, well-spoken, and fond of his little intrigues, but his conception of the depths in play at the Imperial Court could only be superficial, else he would have run screaming into exile long before now.

"And what is my secret?" I said with that practiced smile that gave nothing away, yet promised the moon.

"That your husband does not touch you in your marriage bed," he said. "That you, the most delicate flower in all this cold, hard land, must sustain your soul on the benefits of your high station, and never know the passionate kiss of a man devoted completely to your cause." He touched my arm, and my skin did bunch, but not, perhaps, for the reasons he might presume. The truth was that I had no use for male apparatus in my bed. Elizabeth's sweet tongue had sustained me through my engagement. Now Maria warmed my bed while Peter was off drinking with his friends.

"At least allow me to hope," Sergei said. "Tell me you have not dismissed the possibility entirely from your heart, for I will perish without at least the hope of your affection."

"Hope whatever you wish," I told him. "I have no control over your thoughts."

"Am I not preferable to these men?" He swept his arm to indicate the others in our small court: his ugly older brother, the dashing but empty-headed Niv, and that king of all fools, Monsieur Choglokov, whose only useful skill lay in annually impregnating his wife. "Pompous fools and prissy bootlickers. Surely you prefer my company to theirs."

"You hold rather a high opinion of yourself, sir," I said. "You are married. I am married. Nothing good can come of this."

"Tell me that I am not right, Catherine. Tell me, and I shall be gone forever from your presence." He gave a sly smile. "You will find me splattered across the stones beneath your bedroom window."

If only, I thought. "Spring," I said.

"Spring?"

"Bide your passions until springtime, Sergei. Monsieur Choglokov will invite us to his summer lodge. There, we will certainly find an opportunity to continue this conversation."

"How can you be so sure?" he said. "Monsieur Choglokov's wife will be in labor by then. He will not wish her to travel."

I laughed lightly. "Mademoiselle Choglokov drops children like sweets at a parade. She will be anxious to get away, I assure you." His brows pulled together. I pressed a finger to his lips. "Patience, dear Sergei. I am a Grand

Duchess, not a chambermaid, and must plan these events most carefully."

He nodded, then smiled. "Springtime," he said dreamily, and took his leave. I watched his well-proportioned frame recede, straight back, broad shoulders, thick black hair. For a heartbeat, I let myself see him as he himself had described, sprawled upon the stones beneath my window, blood leaking from his broken skull. That was indeed a possibility, though I must dismiss it. Elizabeth had taught me many things in our time together, but one lesson remained paramount. Murder should not be the solution to every minor annoyance.

In late July, Monsieur Choglokov invited our group to a hunting party on his island in the Neva River. It took very little persuading to get Peter to accept. His eye was on one of Madame Choglokov's ladies, a stump of a woman with a hunched shoulder. No doubt he meant to anger me with this choice, but I was secretly pleased to have him out of my bed as often as possible.

Having banked his desire two or even three months longer than planned, Sergei began his campaign at once. He whispered of love in ways I had not heard, stories of physical passion and spiritual embrace that brought a blush to my cheeks. When his rhetoric rose to the level of pragmatism, and I felt his fingers upon my knee, I put a stop to it.

"And your wife, whom you married two years ago for love? What will she say?"

He shrugged. "All that glitters is not gold. I am paying a high price for one moment of infatuation, I fear."

"And this moment?" I said.

"Ah, my dear Catherine, my feelings for you are as deep as an ocean, more permanent than iron."

"Iron rusts," I told him.

"Not the heart of it," he said, and pounded his chest with such force that Peter looked over. I pretended to appreciate Monsieur Choglokov's poem now being read aloud from the piano across the room. Had Peter possessed even a modicum of sense, he would have known how impossible that was.

The next morning, we set off after the dogs in pursuit of hares. Sergei seized upon his earliest opportunity to corner me on horseback, and spoke freely of the details of arranging a tryst between us. I tried to change our topic to the fine weather and whether boiled rabbit or pelmeni suited his mood for dinner, but he would not be deterred. Finally, I told him that the idea of an affair did please me in an esoteric sense. Mainly I wanted to get Sergei moving again. This long private conversation was bound to draw attention.

"It is settled then," he said. "I have your word." He spurred his horse after the others.

"No!" I shouted after him.

"Yes, yes!" he shouted back.

That evening a gale swept in from the Gulf of Finland, immersing the entire island in water. We were marooned through most of the night. Sergei, of course, took this as a sign from God, and his wooing became even more relentless. Peter and Sergei's brother were drunk, leaving me to defend myself from my suitor's passion.

It quickly became evident that I could not. There is nothing like a day of a horse's shoulders rippling between one's legs to lead one into temptations of the flesh. I devised a plan to bring Sergei into my company that night without suspicion. Peter would be playing cards with the other men and his deformed woman – she was at least their equal in that – and we would have several hours to ourselves.

So it was that Sergei Saltykov sneaked to my room that night in a lady's wig and nightdress to become the first of my male lovers. And, as he did not complain when I commanded him to keep the wig on, this was not the last time we met in bed. For, while a woman's passion demands its succor, a ruler must ever make do.

Bastard!

by Juliet Beckman Hubbell

You are a bastard in every way, Alembert! Odar says you won't get off your Parisian high horse to help me with my crown prince bastard. Even that skulking, beehive-haired mother-in-law of mine doesn't realize how successful Sergei's "surgery" was on Peter's peter. Sergei had to complete two operations on separate patients, a snip there and an injection here, if you follow my meaning. Now you're more *au courant* than your salonnières!

You're oh so holier than the royals I'm slumming with here in Moscow — fine, you're such a philosopher. So then why is it Descartes who had way more cool than you ever will jumped on the first carriage outta town to see that gender-bending, cross dressing freak Christina in Stockholm? He literally died trying to school her and her family, but you can't even make it for a season? Now, post mortem, she's become the darling of all who value reason and morality while I get nothing but grief for doing what comes naturally. By a bastard himself! What's your French expression? *Il n'y a pas de justice*? Damn straight. Frankly, if this kid of mine only needed language tutoring, I'd just send for Denis and his encyclopedia. You share the same office with him; you know he thinks I'm an intellectual hothouse of potential.

So, if bastards are biological (you know why Destouches paid for your education — because your face had the same genetic smirk as he — bastard!), then my son is worth the effort. My son just can't do his maths, and that's where God gave you bastard smarts even if he didn't give you a birthright. Bastard!

And yet here you are, (bastard bastard bastard) and you were able to get the best education available. You make people think that education is what you're all about and you say you're going to make sure everyone gets the same shot as you — but you draw the line at my bastard? Puhleeze. I can't help but wonder if you're not just buying what everyone's selling in spite of your "I'm my own man" crap. We're stuck out here in the freezing hinterland having to beg any French scholar available for help, but you're too busy mulling over your principles to leave your *arrondissement*. Uh-huh.

Maybe it's your innate laziness; isn't that the big complaint about bastards? They have no right to rule and no rules to make right, so they just hang around, writing letters, entertaining friends, living a life of leisure. Come up here and I'll make sure you and your swishy pals have every luxury you need — way more than you'll find in that choking, filthy country of yours. You lazy bastard tutor; can't you see that I am freaking out over this son of mine?

Odar tells me that you also blew off your only contact with my Hohenzollern clan; fine, I get it. That one might come back to bite you. But, they don't have a kid who needs home schooling like my son who seems to have every bizarre behavior possible. You can tell I'm beyond pissed off with you, but this letter should be more semaphore, a flying, snapping banner of a message. You're the best, the very best bastard to better my own (bastard) son. It's urgent. Please come.

Catherine
Moscow, 3 November 1762

Empress
and Autocrat

A Little Squirming

by Matt Potter

He bowed low, looked up at me from beneath peppery eyebrows, and coughed.

"You coughed, sir?" I held his gaze, and smiled.

A crackling fire in the corner had warmed my private study but a chill now hung in the air.

"Sir," I reminded him, "you coughed."

Prince Vasily Steffanoff looked at me longer still, deep and dark, eyes boring into me from the recesses of his craggy face. A favourite once – it was I who gave him his title – our time together since his swarthy looks had faded was now reduced to this daily language lesson. Still, under his gaze I squirmed in my seat. Just a little squirm – my bottom through layers of silk jittering from side to side atop the purple velvet cushion – but a squirm still.

"I coughed because you said go with god, madame," he answered, standing upright.

"Yes," I replied, and smiled again. "I was bidding you adieu."

His hand rose towards the brim of his faded black hat, but then thought better of it so his fingers floated, in mid-air, hat still on his head. "But you said *go with god*. It is something I have noticed of late."

"But as I always do, I said *go with god*, sir. It is a formal greeting of farewell and I employ it often." I looked down again at my Russian homework. I was conjugating the verb *to become involved with fishing* and alas, verb conjugation is, for me, a trial and requires considerable concentration.

Prince Steffanoff stepped toward the escritoire and bent forward, hat bobbing. "You said *go with god*, madame," he whispered. His breath, sour from years of teaching proper and improper nouns, was hot on my face. "You did not say *Go with God*." He stood up and pushed his shoulders back. "And there is a difference."

I sat back in my chair and felt a spasm in my chemise. Of all the days to trial the latest underwear shipped from Madame de Lorgnette in Paris, and I had to pick the one when my Russian teacher chooses to get pernickety about my punctuation.

"But I beg you, sir," I said, standing, the silken skirt-folds of my midnight blue day dress cascading across the verb conjugation on the desk. The back of my knees pushed the half-love seat across the marble floor with a shrill scrape. "I said no such thing."

My heart fluttered inside my ribcage and my eyes blurred, a tactic I often use when confronted with impertinence or logic. Enough doubted my legitimacy to the Russian crown already. As a convert to Orthodoxy and as Empress, I must be pious beyond pious.

"Sir ...?"

"Madame ...?"

46

"… is my private life catching up with me?"

Such a fuss! The screen — sculpted gilt cherubs cavorted across its three panels — stood up with a clatter while, arms folded and bottom cooling through the silk of my dress, I leaned against the marble countertop.

"Only a moment, madame," said the Soup Sous-chef as he directed his staff on how best to arrange the divider. Much arm waving and whispered instructions to his three mop-headed lackeys followed, while he, despite palace etiquette, glanced at me from the corner of both his right eye and then his left.

My patience, sorely-tested, expressed itself in a rhythmic tapping of my heel on the cold stone floor. "Please, sir," I replied. *Tap tap tap.* "My time is yours."

With a modest shove the screen stood ready in place. I slipped behind it and peeling back the imperial tablecloth, uncovered the ingredients.

"The kitchen staff are sure to not disturb you, madame," the Soup Sous-chef said as he took the tablecloth from my arms. "But we are not so far should you need us." And he held out his arm, gesturing behind the screen. My hand caressing a cherub head, I peered behind the divider and through a distant doorway saw another room, filled with kitchen staff and whispered activity.

"Thank you, sir," I said, nodding my head.

"These were all grown in the gardens here at the Catherine Palace —"

I turned away. It's rude, I know, and I should show more interest in my own gardens here at Tsarskoye Selo but I just wanted to get my hands working. *Leave now as I need some thinking time!*

Tap, tap, tap.

The Soup Sous-chef bowed and tipped his white hat. "Go with God, madame."

I opened my mouth to say the same but stopped. "Yes," I said. "And thank you."

My hands dipped into the cooling stock. The juice ran over my fingers and covered up to my wrist, splashing onto the countertop and beading in streaks of brownish-red and reddish-brown and reddish-red and brownish-brown across the marble.

I favour Aunt Olga's traditional recipe.

I don't know who Aunt Olga is, but everyone has an Aunt Olga in Russia so claiming she croaked the recipe to me on her deathbed is something all can relate to.

What is it about making borscht I find so calming?

Wiping my hands on a linen cloth, I picked up the large carving knife with the imperial crest laying beside the large wooden chopping board and speared the large head of the white cabbage. The knife, whisking through the leaves as I cored and chopped and shredded, echoed the thoughts clamouring in my head.

Go with God.

Slice!

Go with God.

Chop!

Go with God.

Shred!

I never feel more Russian than when I am making borscht.

And then I said it aloud. "go with god."

The knife clanged on the marble countertop. Four heads sprang around the screen.

"Madame?" said the Soup Sous-chef.

I grabbed the countertop to steady my shaking legs. "Perhaps today is not the best day for making borscht," I said, leaning against the marble. "My mind is a little distracted."

Four heads nodded. And the Soup Sous-chef looked at me from the corner of his left eye again.

(Once, just once, the Soup Sous-chef had visited my bedchamber late one night with a bowl of *Leberknödelsuppe*, a tender reminder of my childhood in Stettin. Recovering from fever, my thoughts clearing after forty-eight hours of soaking sweats and gibberish, my tears flowed at the sight of the two grey, rounded liver dumplings nestled in beef broth. Alas, the Soup Sous-chef brought only one spoon, but too hungry and too generous for my own good — after the soaking sweats and the gibberish, he caught me at a weak moment indeed — we split the dumplings and sipped the steaming broth from either side of the spoon. And now, I sighed, my own face raised to the ceiling seeking salvation, he thinks he can look at me from the corner of his eye? Oh, surely an empress is allowed just a little undoing?!)

"May I leave this with you?" I said. "My nerves are fractious and my head is spinning." I wiped my hands again on the linen cloth. "Perhaps I will try again tomorrow."

"Of course, madame." The Soup Sous-chef whispered something and the three mop-heads folded the golden screen and leaned it against the wall.

I opened my mouth to thank them but the Soup Sous-chef spoke first. "Go with God, madame," he said. And smiled.

Chin tucked into my cleavage, "go with god," I mumbled. And red-faced with silk rustling, ran through the great kitchen, *tap, tap, tap*. And just as I mounted the first step to make my escape, heard a *snap* as my chemise loosened inside my stays.

Hoiking my skirts to my knees, I slid my leg over the shining black haunches of my favourite steed *Pravda* and stood up in the stirrups. It was long ago, in the reign of Empress Elizabeth, that I stopped riding side-saddle. Twitching the rein, Pravda bolted, my bottom slapping against the leather as we galloped through the Tsarskoye Selo forest, the smell of pine needles and moss in my nostrils, the whip of Pravda's mane against my gloved hands and the thrash of silk skirts pluming behind me.

Through the forest I rode, *Go with God, Go with God* throbbing in my head with each thundering gallop, *Go with God*.

My mind raced. Too many men, too small a bed had always been my motto, but clearly not enough of them had been tied to the Church. Oh, who had stolen my piety without my permission?!

Through a clearing in the forest I saw the blue of the far horizon. If I kept galloping I could make the border in … how many days?

My thighs gripped Pravda's heaving ribs as he thundered beneath me. And my chemise rode with me, each jolt further dislodging it from inside my stays. Soon it covered my cleavage, flapping white against my chin and tickling my cheeks. I jerked on the reins and the horse cantered to a stop. Jumping down, I hoiked up my skirts so I could pull the chemise down from underneath.

"Ahoy, madame."

I jumped and dropped my skirts. "You startled me, sir."

The woodsman stepped forward, moustached and white-toothed under a floppy brown felt hat. "You're having trouble with your chemise." And he reached over as if to stuff it under the neckline of my dress.

Did he know who I was?

He licked his lips. So perhaps he did.

"No, sir," I said. "It is the latest fashion."

"Where?" he asked, eyes twinkling. "Along the Nevsky Prospekt?"

"In Paris, sir," I said, looking down my nose at him and smoothing the chemise's cotton ruffles across my bosom.

"Then madame, I stand corrected. I thought it was only the Empress Catherine herself who could start new fashions, by imperial decree. But by only gazing at you, I know you are quite the fashion-setter yourself and a dangerous rival to the empress in the style stakes." He looked me in the eye, smirked, then bowed his head.

"I try," I said, and eager to make haste, lifted my skirts, placed my foot in the stirrup and swung my leg across Pravda to sit high in the saddle.

And quite forgetting myself, I opened my mouth and said, "go with god."

He looked up. "*go with god*? And is that the latest fashion in all the Russias?"

My bottom, through layers of silk, squirmed atop Pravda's back. Then, "Yes," I said, snapping the reins with my hands. And looking out at the trees and the forest and the clouds and the sky and as far as my eyes could take me, all my own empire, I added, "In all the Russias, yes, it is."

The Cossack Ultimatum

by Gay Degani

As gusts of snow rattled the windows of the Winter Palace, a sly little man scurried through its carpeted halls until he reached a heavy hickory door. He rapped and opened it. "Your highness?"

Catherine glanced up from her needlework, her sharp tongue ready, but when she saw her steward's face, she said, "What is it, Boris?"

"My apologies, your highness. There is a man, a soldier, who is putting it about that he is the godson of Peter." The old man bowed as he eased into the room.

"What do you mean godson of Peter?"

"The first Peter, your highness, the admired one."

"That's ridiculous. Does anyone believe him?"

"They were toasting him with vodka in the streets, your highness."

"What do I care what drunken peasants boast?" Catherine bent to unravel the stubborn knot caught in her thread. Needlecraft calmed her, helped her sort through the burdens of ruling an unruly kingdom at war with the Ottoman Empire.

"He also claims to be the Cossack traitor who led the siege on Bender."

She lifted her head, a smile touching her lips. "Well then, have him arrested and brought to me at once."

"Your highness, the Cossack is below in your courtyard."

With two of her personal guard leading the way, Catherine pulled her ermine wrap tight and strutted outside. White flakes stung her cheeks, snatched her breath, and at first, all she could see was a blur of tussling men. Then the wind died and she found herself staring into dark burning eyes. They held her for a long moment before she considered the rest of him. He was bare-headed in the frozen air, bearded and sharp-boned, manacled between his captors, his thick coat torn open, his tall hat caught beneath his feet. This, she thought, is a rebel and a scoundrel. This is a man.

The guards — it took three of them — shoved their prisoner down, smashing him into the cobblestones with their knees and fists.

"Apologies for the disturbance, your highness!" A lieutenant stepped forward and bending low, he swept his hat to the ground.

"I hear you have captured Monsieur Pugachev?"

"Yes, your highness."

"You have done a great service, the Empress of all the Russias thanks you. You will be rewarded."

Wind shivered through the courtyard, the prisoner turning his bleeding face toward her, eyes defiant. She met them, and said in a harsh voice, "Keep this traitor shackled in the guardhouse until Count Orlov returns from his negotiations with the Turks."

§

"Boris!" she called as she swept into her private apartments.

"Yes, your highness." The steward closed the door firmly behind her. She hurried to her chair, tossed her needlework to the floor, and sat down.

"I have a plan."

When the palace was asleep and the jailers lured away with vodka, her faithful Boris a master of intrigue, Catherine unlocked the door to the Cossack's cell. One of her personal guard set up a brazier in the corner to take away the chill while another dragged in a gold-leaf chair, facing it toward the manacled prisoner. A third hung a lantern from an iron hook on the wall. She dismissed them and settled herself against the chair's soft upholstered back. Adjusted the satin robe around her. She could barely make out the Cossack's torn face in flickering light, but his eyes burned, his chains clinking as he sat up.

"You are Yemelyan Pugachev," she said.

"Your highness, I am that wretched man."

"You say 'wretched' as if it were a blessing. Do not forget I hold your life in my palm." She angled her open hand toward him and snapped it shut. "Perhaps I will use silken ropes to tie your wrists and ankles to my fastest ponies. Put your head on a pike in — what is your village?"

"Zimoveyskaya." He spoke with lightness and pride.

"Zimoveyskaya. A good place for a pike, I should think."

"As you choose, your highness."

"You think you are charming. I can see that." She slipped from her gold chair to hover over him. "Your face is injured, rebel. Does it hurt?"

She stooped and ran a fingernail along the slash in his cheek. He sucked in breath and she smiled, moving her fingers down his neck, scraping, then caressing, then scraping again. The insolence came off him, the male *peasantness* of him too. It stirred her, so she sneered, "You smell like a wounded boar, you know. As if you've been lying in manure."

"Perhaps I have been, your highness, or perhaps I've merely been tending the soil. Voltaire says it is up to us to cultivate our garden, and that is what I am doing since you, Empress, have failed."

"You know Voltaire? You read French?" No mere Cossack this.

He shrugged, his chains clanged. "No, Empress, I cannot read at all, but there are those who spread the words of those who write about the rights of men, and in the south, we have big ears for such ideas."

She was not surprised that he roused her, many men did, but a Cossack was nothing like her usual fare. She was so meticulous about the men she took to bed. She had her ladies try them out. She watched how they performed, rated them, but this was different. Still bending over him, she took one of his chains and tugged at it. Twisted it over in her hand and tugged a little harder.

"Stand up," she commanded and stood a little away from him letting her robe fall open as he struggled to his feet, then

56

she pressed against and felt his readiness. "I have never made love to a dead man before."

"I have never been raped by an Empress before." He had little room to move but he turned her against the wall as she tore at his tattered trousers.

It was not love. It was not rape. It was two bodies, skin against skin, his hunger meeting hers. He could, perhaps, have strangled the air from her lungs, as they came together, his chains jangling, but he didn't, and the danger, the outrageousness, the shift of power, were all part of the thrill.

When she sank, satisfied, into her gilded chair, she said, "You might yet find favor with the second Catherine."

"I seemed to have found favor with her already," he said.

She held out her hand again, palm up, and snapped it closed as a reminder of the absolute power she held over him. "You are in chains. You are a traitor. Do you not value your life?"

It was time to tell him her plan. She was taking a risk — some might say she was committing treason — but how could she commit treason against herself? She *was* Russia. To achieve what she had set out to achieve required patience, daring, and a good deal of luck. She could bring that luck to herself only if she kept her head.

"I have a proposition for you."

"Another one?"

She laid out her plan swiftly, watching the Cossack's face, not knowing when his jailers would return, and knowing her personal guard would be growing restless.

When she was finished he said, "Let me understand, Empress. You want me to continue the rebellion?"

"Yes."

"Encourage the peasants and serfs to join me and the Cossacks?"

"Only to a degree. You must contain the violence as much as possible and stage your battles in areas where you can win — in the disaffected south, on the frontier."

"And for this you will set me free?"

"I will allow you to escape, but you will not be free. You must follow my plan with conviction, but contain it. This will not be easy, but with a little push, Russia's nobility will be forced to give the serfs some small liberties and basic education to understand them. I will insist it is the best way to keep the entire class from rising up against us."

"I have heard it said you are for reform, but excuse me, Empress, this is unheard of, a monarch inciting rebellion."

"I am not inciting rebellion. I am staging it. Do not misunderstand me. I will have armies pulled from the Turkish front to put you down if things get out of hand." She leaned in so he could see the resolution in her eyes. "If you do this, and contain it, and we achieve the results I want, I will reward you beyond measure, and we shall both have what we want."

"You do not know what I want."

"But I do. You and your ilk want autonomy. You want to stay in the borderlands and live your lives. I will leave you and your fellows a certain amount of freedom. You will be a hero, a legend, bringing glory to all Cossacks."

"This is a dangerous, dangerous idea."

"It is, but I want it done. It is not easy to drag this backward country into the enlightened world." She leaned even closer, ice in her voice. "But let me assure you, if you allow this to blow up, I will have you drawn and quartered as you live and decapitated when you are dead."

His eyes did not slide away from hers. "You will free me tonight? Right now?"

"I have the key."

Two Grigorys

by Susan Tepper

Ongoing it is an extremely bitter winter, though all our winters are dastardly cold. My bed is a fortress of misery. Both my Grigorys have been absent past a fortnight, one off waging battle in the western regions, the other laced in the arms of my French cousin, Isabelle, a haughty princess capable of the worst treacheries. Even my little white dog Petrovka developed dripping winter eyes and a hacking squeal-bark. In a fit of abject misery, I strangled the little bitch. Then I placed it on a pillow, tucked in its tail, and it was whisked away by my ladies in waiting. As if it never existed. The way I am feeling, too, useless, pointless; suffering as I am over the absence of my two dear Grigorys: Grigory Orlov and Grigory Potemkin. Or Grigory Potemkin and Grigory Orlov. I have developed an evenness about them, a flat and level plane, though they are vastly different in size and temperament. G.O. is a sensitive soul well schooled in the art of the pianoforte, though his size in trousers and waistcoat leaves something to be desired. While my other, G.P., that virile monster specimen, has taken to abusing large black stallions in the ring. During their joint absences I have grown desolate. I cannot embroider another seat cushion. I cannot partake of the warm liquid that flows out of the steaming samovar. Vodka sipped in solitude bores me to tears. My one Grigory, who likes to whisper *Sophie*, my birth name, into my left ear, moistening my ear folds with his tongue, has left behind a token of himself. A large yellow molar that was extracted shortly before his departure. It smells ripe like an imported cheese. I keep this exquisite part of this Grigory inside my jewel case beside my most opulent diamond tiara. As for my other Grigory, the one I am certain will father several bastards, before his eventual return to this palace, he has left nothing of himself behind but my own deep longing. Today, in a council meeting with my ministers, it was suggested by the dwarf minister, Soleninkoff, that I should exile both Grigorys to the Isle of Elba, where it is reputed others of even higher rank have spent a great deal of pleasant time. I stood at the head of the council table and banged my fist and screamed my disapproval of this plan. Then I sentenced the dwarf minister, Soleninkoff, to death by firing squad. As he was dragged away I felt a certain pleasure sensation, similar to the pleasure that I receive from my two Grigorys. No Queen in any kingdom can quite understand the confusion of two Grigorys. A mix of temptation and despair unlike anything I have encountered, even while riding in battle flanked by the most severe of bodyguards, men who can lop off heads the way peasants lop apples from the trees. But, I am now forced to travel through this winter time alone in my palace. No children or husband to sit with me by the fireside. In solitude I wait, and ponder, wrapped in my sables. I pray with my priests who only wish to see me gone so that the balance of power in my kingdom can be unearthed again. Fools! I will outlive them all!

The Making of a King

by Andrew Stancek

Catherine's hand is on Poniatowski's thigh and her breasts are flushed with bite marks. Poniatowski is still a bull, she thinks, and his stamina, for a man no longer in his twenties, admirable. That stable boy, Kolya, and a steward's son, Efofeyev or some such, they were even more brutish, but among the nobility Poniatowski is unquestionably the champion.

"Marriage," she tells him, "is such a useful tool, Stasik. You know I'd marry you myself but old sourpuss Frederick in Berlin is right. If I marry you, we'll be faced with the wrath of every European ruler. Our delightful gymnastics can continue but we cannot marry." She yawns. Tomorrow she has to meet emissaries from the Ottoman Sultan and Frederick's insufferable minion. She needs sleep but her mind is restless. "Somewhere in the Polish nobility, Stasik, surely we can find a delectable morsel for you to marry? Or would you prefer a Prussian?" She chuckles, as if it were a matter of supreme indifference, but during sleepless nights in her chamber she has entertained fantasies of Poniatowski, King of Poland, by her side as husband, and at their feet, Anna Petrovna, their daughter. Poniatowski has such charm. Bloody vexing she cannot have him even though she is Empress, just because silly rulers are afraid of their common strength.

Poniatowski snorts. He is ready again, monstrous, she sees and reaches for him. No affairs of the state now and no sleep.

At dinner beet juice trickles down her chin as she chomps and sweeps her arm to Poniatowski. "These piss-pots, heads filled with ambition, like noxious bovine gas, are so irritating. Every day some new disaffected claimant, some new conspiracy. This Mirovich, who is he? Man of no money, no influence, no charm. Not even the ability to plot. If he'd had intelligence, he would have known that poor Ivanushka cannot be rescued, cannot have my throne. These shoes pinch me so, Stasik, scratch my foot, will you? The guards had no choice but to kill Ivan at any attempt to free him from Schlusselburg. It might not have been my command, but one issued by my late husband and yet Mirovich, the fool, only brought about Ivan's death. How can you have anything but disdain for such rabble? Now Cherkassov, higher class of fool, wants permission to squeeze the very manhood out of Mirovich, for the names of the other conspirators. Mirovich is no stallion, nothing but a pony, I am told, but I have no desire for torture, no vengeful spirit for offense to my person. The traitor must be punished, of course. Time for new tea in my samovar."

For a moment she gnaws at a pheasant bone, empties her goblet, peers at Poniatowski's profile. "What fine features you have, Stasik, lovely hazel eyes, great eyebrows. Even your head pleases me." Poniatowski licks his lips staring at her, then sticks a fork into his borscht.

"I have it," she says. "After Mirovich's public execution I will have a ceremony — The Unveiling of the Head. It can grace a mace in the ballroom so the fools can see what becomes of conspirators. I will write to Voltaire, see how he likes the idea."

"I will make you King, Stasik," she exhales on a couch in her boudoir later. She bites his shoulder so hard she draws blood. Poniatowski laughs. He lunges at her, buries his face between her breasts. She is a vortex, she thinks. The fate of All the Russias is in her hands. But for now she'll amuse herself with her Polish king, "the king we have made".

Promotion

by Joyce Juzwik

I could not believe my good fortune. One day, I am out in the field with my regiment, guiding new recruits through their daily exercise routine, and the next, I am awaking in the palace of the Empress Catherine, after a full-night's sleep in an actual bed, on perfumed silk sheets. Servant girls brought baskets of fruit, sweets, and pitchers of cold water and placed them next to bouquets of flowers spread throughout the chamber. I felt duty-bound to continue documenting in my military journal, but I hardly knew where to begin.

Field Marshall Grigory Potemkin, rumored to be lover and sole advisor to the Empress, was making his military rounds through the provinces, when he selected several officers in my company to interview privately. I was unaware of any campaigns where my services would be specifically required, but the honor associated with such a meeting eliminated any questions on my part. Whatever task Her Majesty may assign to me, I knew I would perform without a moment's hesitation.

I was helping myself to some fresh fruit – fresh fruit I hadn't had in months – when a young man, close to my age, strolled in, helped himself to a pastry from the silver tray on the beside table and sat down. I was beginning to wonder when an explanation of my current situation would be forthcoming. I was told by Field Marshall Potemkin only that I would be brought to a chamber in the palace where I was to remain until summoned. Perhaps I had been selected to command one of Her Majesty's elite regiments.

"Good morning," he said. "My name is Dmitry. I stay in the chamber at the end of the hallway. You are the third new one to arrive in a week. You probably have a lot of questions as I did, so I thought I'd introduce myself and try to answer some of them for you. We should get acquainted since we'll be seeing a lot of each other in the days to come."

With that, he began to laugh, and leaned over the tray of cakes, poked at a couple of them, then selected one covered in sugar and bit half of it off in one bite. Unfortunately, his words added another layer of mystery to this whole affair. He obviously knew the purpose behind my relocation here, so it likely was not a classified operation. But still, why was I, along with Dmitry and two others, housed within the palace's visitors' chambers?

"Dmitry, I am Alexei. I am a Second Lieutenant with the Artillery. You are a military man also?" I chose to approach the subject gradually in case there was more to this than I had originally anticipated.

"Yes, Alexei, well, I was before I came here. Let me explain. When I was recruited by Field Marshall Potemkin, as you were, I was a Captain in the Infantry. Don't feel obliged to address me as that however, since I no longer function in that capacity, and neither will you."

My confusion must have been obvious, because Dmitry smiled and continued.

"You ... we ... were not selected for our military prowess, my friend. We were brought here to please the Empress. Do I detect a look of puzzlement on your face? Let me be very blunt then. We are here to share Her Majesty's bed and bring her delight to the best of our abilities. Are you shocked?"

I did not want to admit to such a feeling, but being shocked scratched only the surface of the chaos that was now churning in my mind.

"I'm not sure if I'm shocked so much as overwhelmed. I don't understand. Recruited, you say? By the Empress' lover to be her lover? Rather, to be one of her lovers? Actually, the more I explore what you've said, the more shocking it becomes."

Dmitry stretched out on the smaller lounge and continued.

"In truth, the Field Marshall is no longer welcome in Her Majesty's bed. Some sort of conflict with her position, I've heard. But she is not without humanity. Instead of banishing him in disgrace, she elevated him to his present rank and sent him to patrol the provinces of Poland and the areas around the Black Sea. He is currently a Prince of the Empire and resides here at the palace.

"When he is out making rounds of the regiments, he is not doing so to be able to appraise the Empress of their status. He is there to recruit lovers for her, and this is done with her approval. During her marriage to the Grand Duke, she had been denied any sexual favors since his was the mind of a child. After his murder, she took Grigory as a lover, but when his designs on her went beyond the physical, she booted him out of her bed. There was no animosity, but to stay in her good graces, he took it upon himself to provide her with a steady supply of paramours. And so, here we are."

I could not believe what I was hearing. Hijacked from my regiment by a token Commander to demean myself by catering to the sexual demands of my Empress, who by now has to be in her 50's at least.

"Oh, I almost forgot," Dmitry continued with a smirk. "You'll be examined by the Court's physician to ensure you are free from disease, then taken to the chamber of the Countess Bruce for a try-out."

His hearty laughter at his last remark caused my face to flush hot with embarrassment, as I attempted to convince myself he would not next offer a description of how the elder Countess planned to test the proficiency of my virility.

"A try-out? What does that mean?"

"Just what it sounds like, my friend. The Countess will explain Her Majesty's sexual preferences, and you will be expected to enact them with the Countess. If she is pleased, you will be approved for contact with the Empress. It's the way things are done here."

I was appalled. So, I was supposed to be auditioned like an actor for a role? Then what? Kept here against my will and expected to perform on the whims of my Empress? This was something I could not abide. Along with the fact that this sinful display of allegiance to my Empress strayed far from the rigid code of morality I adopted as a youth, the image in my mind of Her Majesty's pale and wrinkled body under mine caused this morning's tasty treat to rise to the back of my throat. I feared, however, that there was only one way out.

"This may be acceptable to you and the others, but it is not for me. In all good conscience, I cannot commit myself to such a distasteful existence. Should I refuse, however, I will be taken out and publicly executed. Correct?"

Dmitry stood up and filled a goblet with some of the sweet scented water and handed it to me.

"Relax, Alexei. You couldn't be more wrong. Let me tell you how this works. Should you accept this duty, you will be handsomely paid after each lovemaking session and also, this chamber will remain yours until such time as you tire of your role here or the Empress replaces you with another. Either way, at that time, you will no longer be allowed in the palace, but will have been paid enough to find another suitable home elsewhere.

"If, though, you choose to refuse outright, there will be no execution. Again, you will not be permitted to enter the palace, but you will receive payment sufficient to continue your life in some other profession. Returning to your regiment will be out of the question, but there are other careers, and with enough money to sustain you for a long period, you can take your time choosing one.

"It is, in my eyes, a win either way, but frankly, Alexei, I'm glad I chose to stay. At times, it is just she and I, but on other occasions, she summons us all to her chamber. It gets quite interesting then."

All? At the same time?

"Oh, Alexei, I should tell you. When there are three of us, only one makes love to Her Majesty. The Empress then commands the other two to have sex with each other while she watches. Still interested in leaving?"

He smiled, placed his hand on mine and gave it a light squeeze before he left for his own chamber. A servant girl came to let me know my presence was requested by the Countess Bruce. And, so it begins. Come to think of it, with me here now, there is the potential for four of us to be called to Her Majesty's chamber. Hmmm...

For the honor of my country, I shall do my duty as required. As challenging as this new phase of my life may become, I shall endeavor to endure.

Baobabs

by L.S. Johnson

Every day, when the clock chimes three, the little Frenchman comes to her, and they close the door, and they talk.

Catherine understood from the beginning it would be like a love affair: the rush of infatuation and then the slow crescendo of little disappointments. She understood that much as a woman. She understood, too, that this was a rare opportunity, perhaps her only such: to wring the mind of one of the great French *philosophes*, to wring him dry, and all for the price of a library.

She understood that as an empress.

She wanted to immerse him in Russia, in the problems of Russia, to bring to bear all his thought on her singular country. She understood that he would want to immerse her in France, in his own philosophy, the better to mold her into the ideal autocrat he and Voltaire imagined.

She understood that as a matter of tactics, and she brought her needlework to the room each day, her head bowed demurely as the great Diderot spoke.

Tactics.

Diderot tells her: *the basis of spoken authority is not a crown or a sword, but science and good faith, enlightenment and sincerity.* So earnest his cheeks are flushing. To make his point he taps her thigh, *science*, and again, *sincerity*, so hard she feels as if he has touched her very skin, as if the layers of silk and damask have broken beneath his small round fingertip.

And she thinks, my God, what if I had come before Peter with nothing on my person but a book of science and goodwill? Then we would be speaking German, not French, all beneath the Prussian flag – and that presumes I would be alive at all, and granted enough freedom to speak to another.

Authority comes from education, he says, tapping her again. *Speak factually and honestly and you will be able to sway any audience, for they will sense your authority, far more than any display of arms . . .*

But she has stopped listening, because he does not understand. Education, yes: she dreams of a day when she might listen to an educated parliament legislate her realm in rational terms, from prince to serf. But now, when there are whole regions that would not know her from a washerwoman? Such subtleties would be wasted. Her vast country demands vast displays: grand palaces, cathedrals scraping the heavens, gleaming rifles as far as the eye can see.

That is *authority* in Russian.

The Frenchman's hand on her thigh, the weight of him beside her. She has a sudden, absurd vision of embracing him, his soft round face between her breasts, her skirts hiked past her waist like the girl she never was. Is this how he woos his lovers? With little taps on the legs, *open up my girl, science demands it, can't you see I'm sincere?*

With a careful twist of the thread she forms a little petal, and stitches it in place, raising her hoop to hide her smile.

He tells her: *you should teach every Russian girl basic human anatomy, so they can better keep their lovers, and fend off ravishment.*

She is momentarily disconcerted - teach anatomy to girls? how many of them could even read? - then, considering, she looks at him slyly over the curved edge of her embroidery hoop. *Why, Monsieur! Have my ladies disappointed you?*

And he laughs, a hearty guffaw that she did not know he possessed, and squeezes her arm. *Marvelous, my good woman,* he praises. *You would be at ease in any salon in Paris.*

His hand on her arm. The plain suits he has worn since arriving, their seats rubbed to a shine; she had thought herself done with men in rough linen. What had seemed a charming disregard for custom is now starting to resemble mere affectation.

Has he been playing, then, when he completes his afternoon audience? Roaming the halls of her palace, freed from obligation? Certainly he wouldn't want for entertainment. So many bright-eyed girls at court now, lithe and pretty, easy with their smiles and their favors. As she herself would never be, now. She knows every line on her face, she can feel herself thickening and slowing. All her power and she cannot take back a few precious years.

Now the fruit of the African baobab, he tells her, *is noted for its ability to regulate a woman's courses and cleanse the blood of illness, with far more success than mere bloodletting. I have prepared a paper for you on the subject.*

Another disconcerting statement, that takes her a long moment to understand; and then it is her turn to laugh outright, letting the hoop fall into her lap. *But Monsieur*, she says, laughing still, *how in God's name do you know such a thing? I did not think you were so widely traveled.*

Books, he admits proudly. *We are living in a new Alexandria, Madame. All man's learning can be known by merely opening a volume; and the measure of a man and a nation alike is the library they possess. As you know, for I have seen your own collection. It is testament to your fitness to rule, and through you it will become the glory of Russia.*

She picks up the hoop again, her smile fading. Her little *philosophe* is lying now, though he may not know it. Books could only speak of symptoms, not sensations; they recorded quantifiable phenomena, not what lay within.

Her best years wasted in a cold bed, shunned and ignored, thinking always on Russia, Russia, how best to serve Russia. Sent to another's bed like a whore, thrown over like a whore, all for Russia. Her babies birthed and spirited away, for Russia. Her own neck nearly on the block, for Russia. All that she had risked: for Russia. Never to be transcribed, never to be given freely to any idiot browsing a bookshelf.

That was the measure of Catherine.

She thinks: I have bought myself a reader, nothing more. All his ideas, all his writings, all based upon books and conversation. Never upon application.

She thinks: I would go to Africa in a heartbeat. Oh, would that I could have been a man! Where, in this vast world, with all its wonderful creations – where is the fruit for that?

My good woman, he begins – and he is serious now, like a papa addressing a child – *my good woman, the most important thing for you to understand is your own power: from whence does it come? What shapes its character?*

She looks at him sideways, and stabs her needle hard into the fabric. *I am listening, Monsieur.*

She does not add, I once had a father, and you are not he.

Diderot tells her: *every prince upon this earth derives his power from his people. Now men are free or slaves, and Nature makes the latter to encourage virtue in the former; but the nation is made of free men, and it is through contract with them that a man – or a woman – has the authority of the crown.*

Catherine makes a careful backstitch, and another, neatly splitting the threads.

Now the character of your power is based foremost upon your aristocracy, your noblest subjects. They are your democracy, and as long as they are virtuous Russia will be strong and powerful.

And she nearly says, Monsieur, have you really seen us? Any of us? And have I really seen you in turn? For France must be a quaint little country to inspire such ideals, with its virtuous nobility, its borders as close and cozy as a nice settee. While I must govern Russians and Poles, Cossacks and soon the Turks as well if God wills it; all these men and more than half in serfdom – and most cannot write their own names. What would they do to me if I went prancing about the countryside, preaching these ideas? They would kill me, swiftly and without hesitation.

That is our contract.

I reign over barbarians, she nearly says. Your ideas play well here, on my silk sofa, before the warmth of my hearth, your belly full of my wine and food. But you try them out there, Monsieur, and see how far you get.

He is nattering on in his nasally French, his finger tapping her thigh again and she winces: so many touches now upon her person, she is bruised.

She thinks, I am the victim of my own pride. Voltaire, Diderot, Grimm, they all flatter me – but they flatter Sophie the lonely bookworm, not the Empress Catherine. And Sophie is long dead.

And when next the clock chimes three the needlework has disappeared. Catherine sits upright, and gestures to the chair across from her. The chair is at arm's length, and there is a small table positioned carefully between them, as solid and as absolute as a throne.

First of a Fine Spectacle

by Robert Mangeot

Katerina hooded her gaze. "La Harpe told you everything?"

Her footman intoning "Katerina the Second, Empress and Autocrat of All the Russias," still dizzied me even after it no longer echoed through her salon. My endless bow had me near toppling over, blood pounding in my ears. I, the librettist known for his single glorious failure, had been dragged into a private audience with the Empress herself.

"I'd have us speak plainly." Katerina said. "Mr. Nowicki, are you quite well?"

I was not. My business in Saint Petersburg, to discuss texts for the soon-to-open Bolshoi Opera, had ended badly. Before I could present my tragedy *Kristall-Herzen*, about a fortune teller in love with her destined murderer, La Harpe made clear the true commission: to supervise texts credited to Empress Katerina. We debated the matter, he considering it an honor and I a prison sentence to be shunted into a ghost-writer's closet. In that sense I won the argument when imperial guardsmen hauled me away.

"Mr. Nowicki?"

Katerina stood beside the piano, her face a once-perfect egg now swollen by age, her dark blue eyes still dancing with intelligence. Her white gown glowed in the sunlight surging through the windows. Outside the river flowed oblivious to my plight.

"Mr. Nowicki, I am accustomed to having my questions answered."

"Pardon me, Empress. Anonymous collaboration, he called it."

Katerina stared me down like a lioness choosing her supper. "Artur Nowicki. You're Polish. You're not hoping to kill me, are you?"

I wondered the same about her. Abduction had that effect on me. Luckily, no one invented narrow escapes quite like a librettist. I would construct a fake demise, one set on a time delay thanks to some obscure and vaguely fatal disease. "I'm not political. Even if I had the strength."

"Because I won't apologize. Russia had territorial claims, and I pursued them. It's why they gave me the job."

"Again, that's beyond my depth."

"Nymphs in a Russian wood."

I nodded and used the moment to adjust my collar. Nymphs at the Hermitage made no less sense than disgraced librettists. Who knew what the Empress of All the Russias had running about the place?

Katerina swept a hand toward the piano. "An idea I'm toying with. Make me hear nymphs in a wood."

"Might we discuss my situation?"

"Nymphs."

I edged onto the piano bench, Katerina stepping in behind me, the unblinking stares of the plasterwork cherubs weighing on my shoulders. Nymphs would caper, and so I started my right hand on a jaunty allegro. I recalled the forests along the ride from Warsaw, the mad growth of summer, lichens and deer and dappled sun, and brought my left hand in to harmonize a dark rhythm.

"Stop!"

I drew back from the keys, my shoulders lighter despite Katerina's hovering shadow. A poor showing could be blamed on my advancing disease.

"I'm not at all certain that wood was Russian," Katerina said. She settled beside me on the bench. "Artur, I'm Sophie."

"Empress?"

Katerina shot me a grin. "No more Empress, please. Not in session. How do you propose declaring my ideas crap while calling me Empress?"

"Well," I said, inching away while my tongue found courage, "Sophie, you are perhaps too hard on yourself."

"That's what Voltaire said. He never managed a decent libretto, did he? So out with it. The verdict on my nymphs from Artur, the genius of *Die Verwunderung*."

My only text ever staged. My blessing, my curse, and not even my best, nothing like *Kristall-Herzen*. "It flopped."

"The production flopped. Your writing was brilliant. A true voice, essentially unheard. There it is. Now, when you were playing the nymphs, something held you back. Was it the nymphs or the wood?"

Both, though I found my abduction more distracting.

"Plain speaking, Artur. If you believe nymphs are shit, then say so."

Surely that truth doomed me as much as the fortune teller in my masterpiece. "Plainly, I am not right for the job. My health is in fast decline, I fear."

"Here we go again. Please know I'm not sorry."

I had expected more difficulty faking, and perhaps a morsel of sympathy for, my condition. Regardless the bright prospects of freedom and redemption shimmered around me. "I am grateful for your understanding."

"I meant about Poland. If you expect me to say it was all Potemkin's idea, I shall disappoint you. It was mine, and I would do it again without hesitation." Katerina — Sophie — wheeled to face the keys, the drapes of her gown rustling against me. "Were you in the war?"

With the speedy Russian victory, the closest thing to violence I experienced as an infantryman was mild dysentery. Something like it rumbled in my gut now at freedom's light flickering. "I was."

"Good you made it through." Sophie turned to the keyboard again and played a snippet of my capering theme, her technique precise if flat, but her fingers dwelled over each note as if deliberating it, showing it respect. "Stop putting distance between us, Artur. I've done my part setting you straight about Poland. Now let's have the same from you."

I wiped sweat off my palms. For my escape, for my masterpiece *Kristall-Herzen*, I intended a fraught tale of mere weeks to live. Some power in her blue eyes trapped the lie in my chest. "I worry nymphs are not ideal for opera. In my opinion."

"Hardly. They're putting on a play. About what I haven't decided, but only the most beautiful get the plum parts."

An idea no more operatic than dysentery. Frustration blazed through me, my skin prickling with its sparks. "And yet the dramatic potential seems limited. A text must free the composer and performers to emote."

"You see it. Exactly what trips me up. I'm always short on conflict." Sophie continued my caper melody, adding notes for texture, building it until with great flourish she pounded a bass chord that shuddered through the salon. "A satyr."

At least fate granted my fortune teller the release of death. Sophie chained me and my redemption to nymphs and satyrs. "Such a gift for opera certainly doesn't require my services."

"I'm from Pomerania, you know. Originally. Lovely country, practically Poland. So. We'll need a deliciously evil name for our satyr."

"Nymphs are shit." The words burst out before I could catch them. The anger and fear that bubbled out from me kept digging my grave. "And you had me hauled in like a criminal."

What hung between us seemed the quiet between the drums and the falling axe.

"Ah, plain speaking," Sophie said. "Watch as I return your volley. Nymphs are beyond shit. I wouldn't put my name to nymphs if it earned me Sweden. What if we adapted a folk tale? With a dragon?"

I stood and straightened my jacket. "Arrest me if you will," I heard myself say, "but I must decline your commission. My creations deserve my name."

Sophie heaved a sigh. "Oh, all right. I'm sorry. Not for the war. But that you and so many had to fight in it. Merciful heavens, see what you've won from me?"

I had won nothing but a dragon. My resolve buckled, and I crumpled back down on the bench. "I don't need an apology. I need my work, to have my voice heard. You won't buy me with money."

"Of course not."

"And especially not trying to flatter *Die Verwunderung*. To be heard once hurts worse than never."

"I'd call that sentimentalist twaddle coming from anyone other than you. Someone to undo me so easily into apology knows the tragedy is not to be heard at all. What about magic wheat?"

"Pardon?"

"For our folk opera. We'll find someone for the score sure to pack a house. Having The Empress and Autocrat of All the Russias involved won't hurt, either." Sophie leaned over, filling my nose with the orange-scented powder in her hair. "They'll hear Artur and Sophie all the way in Vienna."

Finally I saw the method lurking behind her crooked grin. Sophie — Katerina — wanted us both to be heard, her through me, me through her. She brought me there to make clear my choice: Warsaw or Saint Petersburg, the dream to be heard truly or the certainty to be heard well.

"Dragons are hard to stage," I said. "What about this? A fortune teller divines her true love will someday murder her."

"It's a start." Katerina rose, drawing me up with her. "You're a crafty one, Artur. A master of silences and player of long games. Tomorrow you shall not take me by surprise."

Empress Katerina turned, and I bowed in her wake as she swished out of the salon. The craft on display had not been mine.

Crowning Achievement

by Gill Hoffs

The crown stinks of dead people, but I don't mind. It distracts my senses from the squalor of our hut and the waste seeping from the ruin beneath the blankets. Urine trickles off the piss-yellow straw poking from my mattress and splashes on the floor. My father scrapes crescents of grime from the tips of his nails, one hand caressing the other as he pretends not to watch me handle the old gold headwear and I pretend not to notice the bottle missing from the shelf beside the fire.

When I was a little boy, my brothers and I called them wish-bottles. At first we put notes in them, wishes for amazing items written on scraps of paper or the largest leaves of the laurel, pale green, stiff, and shiny, pulled from the tree by the bridge. Blue leather shoes with singing laces. A bird's nest made of sugar. A dog that shat stew and dumplings.

We would plug the bottles with twigs and mud, or wax, then throw them in the stream and watch the sunlight sparkle on the glass as they bobbed down to the reed beds. Any that passed safely through would come true. Those hesitating beside the bulrushes were collected, their wishes discarded, the bottles rinsed and replaced by the fire once again. As we grew older, we used them for other kinds of wishes; mainly I

Owe You notes switched for items pilfered from markets and the wealthier estates, a wish in this case that we could somehow pay them back. My parents put a stop to that when Yuri was locked up for swapping a wish-bottle for a pheasant, the fool's signature damning him to detention far away.

But now it's just my father and I and the woodlice escaping from the logpile by the door. My father has run out of nails to clean and is cracking his knuckles as I fondle the old gold. The metal warms in my hands and I rub old lady dust from the writing at the front.

EKATERINA

I doubt anyone will find the bottle, in my lifetime or his. The dead of Peter and Paul Cathedral can decay in peace, disintegrate into cold broth and bones within their marble tombs with no further interruption from workmen like my father. My departure is one of heat and wet suppuration but I imagine those corpses in their metal coffins and brocade finery, imagine them withering and draining until nothing but bones, hair, and dresses float in a pool of what they once have been.

"It's beautiful."

The corners of his smile lift swags of cheek below eyes the rich colour of peat. His eyes match his teeth. My father is ageing towards death but will outlive me, I'm sure. Although the gold is heavy and my scalp sensitive to every hair's direction and each insect's bite, I place the crown over my curls, then lean my head back into the blankets and pull the longest ringlets down over my chest.

My mother had curly hair like mine, and as the youngest I had her attentions with the comb after dinner every night. The songs of strength and glory, the tales of bear hunts and wise women, were for my brothers, not for me. Instead, mama crooned of love and frogs, armless maidens and strange children, and told me of the time she saw Catherine the Great sail past on the river.

The empress was in her favourite pale clothing, white velvet and silver brocade puffed like a cloud rained down from the heavens. Her hair was so dark and lustrous it left all who saw her yearning for treacle, the blondes in our village dipping their tresses in henna and stewed tea, striving for royal perfection. She met my father on the riverbank when he stood on her foot, the crowd pushing them together, treading irises and daisies into the mud as the royal fleet sailed on. We miss her still.

I suck my lips in over my teeth, the loose white squares scraping, swelling, and darkening the flesh so I can pout and look the part. He always wanted a daughter, but baby after baby was born with a penis and welcomed with a sigh.

I watched lambs lose their tails to ribbons while springing across pastures dappled with buttercups and speedwell. Thought about my father, chose a length of ribbon, and wound it round, tight.

But I am not a sheep.

Fever brings sweat to my forehead, and the crown slips a little closer to the plucked lines of my eyebrows. My cheeks are flushing, I can feel their heat, and I look up at my father as he clasps his hands close to his chest, his posture telling me he's pleased. I smile a little, careful to keep my lips pushed out and full, and ask in my softest voice: "Is this crown fit for your princess?"

He nods, eyes nestled in wrinkles and full of shiny water. "It's a crown that fitted an empress."

Favourites

by Anne Scott

Catherine – blurred and smudged, smoky with age. My vision has only memories for sight. They offer themselves to me in a miasma of mystery, obscuring my view with the vagaries of time. The capricious nature of ageing and its greedy lust for time has left me with lovers' faces, misted and vague.

If I had a painter's hand, could I sweep my fine sable brush with the caressing touch of a lover's hand? Would my canvas receive the strokes of erotic excitement … the blush of colour? Could it suck at the salty residue of paint or hear the cacophony of sound as the strokes become a symphony that dances to the little death?

But my dance partners are now only arcane shadows. Do I know whether to frown or smile or cry out in passion? Oh, Peter, Alexander, Serge, Stanislaw, Pyotz or Grigory Orlov! Each lover a different course, our appetites metabolising a feast of the erogenous. The ghosts of the living and dead swirl and focus only to mist and outline in colours of blue and grey, charcoal and ebony, their faces distorted with anguish and the grief of time.

Ah! But Grigory Potemkin. I do not need the shadows of memory to recall you – because my heart does – your laughter, your wit, your charm, forever you; our greedy lust waltzing us to the messianic deliverance of the little death again and again and again. But not this time Grigory ... this time I dance in the shadow of death itself.

Is that you I see coming towards me, hand outstretched for mine? The ballroom glitters in brilliance and gold. The silk of fine dresses press against the golden emblems of uniforms, as the sultry thighs of men claim their partners. The diamonds at my neck reflect your image as the ballroom dancers send back their vision in my circling earrings.

We swirl and reverse side-step and circle, eyes coupled in embrace. I dare not look down at your calf-covered thighs. Or watch your steps as they entwine in mine. Or hear the cadence of music as you sweep and swing me to its tempo, your hand pressed to my back as my barely-covered breasts moisten and gloss.

Oh Grigory – is that you leaning against my canopied bed requesting admittance? My handsome, brilliant lover framed in your Hussars' uniform inviting me to draw back the bed-covers. Oh Grigory, we have sinned and twisted as in the waltz. But I have changed partners. My only dance partner now is death. The only cover – a shroud. My bones are chastened by pain, my flesh wasted. Death hovers and will not be denied. Is that you calling out to me, Grigory?

'Behold the eye of the Lord is upon Thy servant Catherine in this hour of her death.'

The prayers of the gathered priests modulate the death chant. 'Her soul waits for your forgiveness, mercy and love O Lord.' Incense burners rhythmically swing high and low besmirching the already sullied death air of the room.

'To Thee, O Lord I lift up the soul of Thy servant Catherine. My God in Thee we trust. Let not the enemy of death triumph over her. Shepherd her through the valley of the shadow of death.'

With the cup of holy oil clasped in his hand, the Patriarch leans over Catherine and anoints her head with oil. Making the sign of the cross he murmurs to her. *'Hear me O Lord. Through your unfailing love, grant Thy servant Catherine peace in her time of tribulation and mercy that she may dwell in your house forever.'*

Catherine – Is that your hand reaching out, Grigory? I'd love to dance.

and then some

The Kings and I

by Kim Conklin Hutchinson

Yes, history does repeat itself. From up here, it's a bit like watching oneself in a play … over and over. It's fascinating how one little Prussian woman can become the source of so many passionately believed rumours, innuendos, and outrageous legends.

It wasn't as if I did anything other empire builders don't do all the time, and haven't throughout the ages. It's just that I sought out willing sceptres, rather than having possessed one of my own.

Throughout history, other women had also ruled alone, and one even died a reputational virgin. But me … Well, ask a few ladies-in-waiting for a little dating help, maybe to audition a few potential booty calls, and the prospect of a courtly stud farm suddenly becomes being crushed to death during an assignation with a horse.

History isn't fair. Neither is life. My real death was even more undignified, a form of passing that I share with another kind of later monarch, the king of rock-n-roll.

I'll admit that I was no ingénue. I'd detested my husband since childhood. Even then, I knew he was a drunkard on our first meeting, but I was sold off by my *noble* family, in particular, my icily ambitious mother. But, I learned my way 'round the court, in both the front and back rooms, and finally retired to my chambers to bide my time.

It came. The world went to war for seven years, a biblical flood of chaos and destruction, and my silly king chose the wrong side. He would see my homeland divided, which I could not stand for, and conveniently, he turned all of his nobles against him. So he stood alone, and he left me in the capital ... also alone, and free to plan his dethroning. Soldiers fall in struggle of battle. So do kings.

Once the throne became mine, I turned out to be a much more talented regent. I brought the West and East together, forming a bridge. Then, the same year that England lost a large part of her prize, when the colonists declared their independence, so did I. My passion for my lover had cooled, and instead of quietly retiring to a large estate, he suggested he might be of more help to me in court, procuring and vetting new entertainments for my enjoyment. The world was upside down with change. Why not? I thought. I'd brought art, culture, wealth and many new ideas to my kingdom. I'd transformed Russia and proven myself on the geopolitical stage. It only seemed reasonable to reward myself with a few private, offstage pleasures.

Why not, indeed. My romantic drama didn't stay offstage long. All of my accomplishments were soon overshadowed by the gossip. I became a laughingstock, the butt of crude jokes, another thing I share with that later bejeweled ruler, he the lover of black hair dye, jumpsuits and PB and banana sandwiches. I could have told him, Mr. PB+B, how the high life would end, ignominiously, in a most undignified evacuation –

an episode that I'm also forced to view again and again, on an endless loop — but there's no long distance service from here to there.

True, it all was a very long time ago, and maybe I should get over it already. But it's not that easy. It was my only life, and I tried so hard to make it mean something, to make a positive impression on the world, and leave my part in better shape that I found it. Perhaps, especially after all this time, I shouldn't complain about the crushing legend. Given the option, it's at least a more glamorous ending. But how sad that what should have been a heroic herstory comes down to being remembered most for something that did or didn't happen at one of my lower orifices or the other, and in that limited range of choices lies the true tragedy.

A Horse's Tale

by Todd McKie

Lucy loves costume parties. I hate them. I'm perfectly content to be myself, psychological warts and all, but Lucy craves the chance to be someone else, if only for a few hours. That's the reason we went to the Abbotts' Halloween party as Catherine the Great and Her Horse. Lucy laid a guilt trip on me: "Why can't we ever do something I want to do?" she said.

I can't stand the Abbotts, Lyle especially, and I certainly didn't want to spend hours at their place dressed as a fucking horse! But I wasn't going to say that. I agreed to go if Lucy made my outfit — she's the creative one.

Lucy made a tiara out of cardboard and tin foil. She bought a bagful of glass 'gemstones' and glued them onto the tiara. Lucy already had a gown, one she claims her great-great-grandmother wore to a fancy ball at the Plaza just before the Depression.

Moths had gotten at the gown, but Lucy said it didn't matter, Harriet Abbott had promised to turn the lights down real low. I said, "Yeah, but will they be low enough so I look like a real horse?"

When Lucy finished her costume she bought me a brown turtleneck jersey and brown tights. She made the horse's back end out of paper maché, with a mop for a tail. Lucy made a penis for the horse by stuffing one of her nylons with shredded newspaper and stapling it between the horse's legs. She made a horse head with a long neck and big ears. I thought the ears looked more like rabbit ears than horse ears, but I didn't say so.

I tried on the costume. The head was heavy and it got hot inside real fast and the eyes were in the wrong places. The back end of the horse was fastened around my waist and its legs scraped against the floor. I felt like I was dragging a wagon behind me.

"Move around," Lucy said. "Let's see if you can dance in it."

Dance? I could barely walk in it. Shuffling around our living room I knocked over a lamp. Lucy made the eye holes bigger, but it was still difficult to see where I was headed.

"We're going to look so great together!" she said.

"You're going to look great," I said. "I'm going to look like an asshole."

One night a few days before the party I was watching TV when Lucy walked in and handed me a paperback book: *Catherine the Great: Russia in the Age of Enlightenment.*

"Read it," she said.

"Why?"

"Research."

I skimmed through the book and learned some interesting facts: Catherine wrote an autobiography, an opera, essays on womanly virtues, and a cookbook. She invented an irrigation system — viaducts, tunnels, and pumps — to supply water to farms all across Russia. Catherine gave every Russian family a free book and a lamp to read it by. The book, an abridged version of her autobiography, was dedicated to

All the Children of Russia,
that You may Better Appreciate
your Homeland's Glorious History
and True Destiny.
— Catherine, Exalted Mother of All Russia.
St. Petersburg, 1767.

People were grateful for the lamp, but because most Russians were illiterate, the book's pages were mostly used as toilet paper, replacing, briefly, corn husks, leaves, and clumps of hay.

Catherine, it turns out, wasn't even Russian. She was German. Her mother tricked her into marrying dim-witted Prince Peter of Russia when Catherine was fifteen years old. Peter was a spoiled brat who suffered from erectile dysfunction, so Catherine slept around — people whispered that she was a nymphomaniac, and worse: there were rumors about her and a horse.

Whoa! That caught my attention.

Catherine organized a coup against poor, goofy Peter, who ended up dead, leaving her to rule the Empire. Historians still disagree about the horse thing, some insisting the rumors were part of a plot to discredit Catherine, declare her insane, and install Peter's younger, smarter brother as Emperor.

On the morning of the party Lucy called in sick and spent the whole day getting ready. When I returned from work her hair was braided and full of tiny ribbons, her cheeks were red, and she had a large black mole beside her mouth.

I said, "What's with the mole?"

"It's not a mole, it's a beauty mark. Moles have hairs growing out of them."

I pulled on the turtleneck and tights. I put on my clunky brown shoes. Lucy got into her gown and fastened the tiara atop her new hairdo with bobby pins.

"Look what Janet loaned me," Lucy said, holding up a riding crop. She started swatting me with it. She was just fooling around, but it really stung.

"Jesus," I said, "that hurts!"

Lucy wanted me to drive to the party wearing the head. She said, "It'll help you get into character."

"Into character?" I said. "I'm supposed to be a horse, for God's sake!"

While Lucy, who'd become Catherine the Great, settled herself regally in the car, I threw the horse head and hindquarters into the back seat.

The party was going strong when we arrived. After struggling up the steps leading into the house I ran smack into Lyle Abbott, dressed as a yachtsman in green slacks, topsiders, and an admiral's cap. Lyle slapped my flank and said, "Welcome aboard, Mister Ed!"

While her friends admired Lucy's costume I trotted down the hallway in search of alcohol, colliding with zombies, a football star, a vampire, and a woman who said she was Steven Tyler. I staggered into the kitchen, took off the horse head, and wiped my sweaty face with a paper towel. I poured myself a big glass of wine. I asked Phil Palmer, who wasn't wearing a costume — just a huge pair of glasses with wide black frames covered in rhinestones — who he was meant to be.

"I'm supposed to be a guy having a mid-life crisis," said Phil.

"Oh," I said, "the glasses, huh?"

"Yeah, sort of. I dunno, is it stupid?"

"You're asking a guy dressed up like a horse if your costume is stupid?"

I was guzzling my third glass of wine when Catherine came in looking for her horse.

"There you are," she said. "C'mon, let's dance." I put the head on and followed her to the living room. The Abbotts had pushed back their furniture and taken up the rugs. Hillary Clinton and Spiderman, Popeye and Lady Gaga, along with several other couples, were dancing to 'It's Raining Men', by the Weather Girls. Catherine pulled me onto the dance floor.

I did my best, but I kept crashing into people and stomping on their toes. I was dizzy, out of breath, and my head was on fire. Catherine slapped me with her riding crop, ordering me to "dance faster!" and "feel the music!"

That's when I tripped and fell, smashing my hindquarters. I lay there wondering if I could get up — my shoulder hurt like hell. Popeye pried off my head and unhooked me from what remained of my rear end. Abe Lincoln came over and helped me to my feet.

Lucy was concerned: Was I okay? Did I break anything? But then she was Catherine again, scowling and saying, How could a horse be so clumsy?

Donna Summer was singing 'She Works Hard for the Money', but I didn't want to dance anymore – I wanted to go home. I sat on the sidelines nursing my aching shoulder and watching Catherine dance with Popeye the Sailor Man. President Lincoln brought me a plateful of grilled shrimp, dipping sauce, and potato salad.

I dozed off. When I woke up the music had stopped, the lights had been turned up. Sarah Palin, the zombies, Big Bird, Power Ranger, and Liza Minnelli were saying their goodbyes, thanking Harriet and Lyle, raving on about what a great party it had been. "Maybe we should make this an annual event!" said Lyle.

Back home I couldn't wait to get in bed and go to sleep, but Catherine had other plans. She slipped a hand inside my tights. "Horsey, do me a favor, okay?"

"What now?"

"Keep your costume on, your shoes too, and put on the head."

I refused to put on the head, but I climbed into bed wearing my turtleneck, those stupid tights, and my shoes.

Catherine switched off the light and, still in her gown, crawled in beside me.

It wasn't without its logistical complications — the shoes, the gown, the shoulder — but, yes, Catherine the Great did have sex with a horse.

Cannon-Firing Noises

by Dusty-Anne Rhodes

"Upon her marriage, Catherine found herself shackled to a 17-year-old"[1] whom one European king would remember as 'a mere poltroon[2] ... comic in all things ... not stupid, but mad.'"[3]

"It was discovered that all Peter did at night in bed with Catherine[4] was play with wooden soldiers, miniature cannons and toy fortresses. Peter would make little cannon-firing

---

[1] As we grow older, the image of being shackled to a 17-year old (so long as the shackles are not excessively uncomfortable) can sound like a rather delightful fate. But as a 15-year old Anhaltinian princess in an era when noble women were merely pawns in larger-scale power games, the situation was no doubt quite different.

[2] Even the well-read may not be familiar with the term 'poltroon', although whatever it is - (A flimsy raft on a lake, or rather a marine floating structure? No, that's a 'pontoon'. A caricature intended to make us chuckle? No, that's a 'cartoon'. A term from old New Orleans describing a person of one-quarter black ancestry? No, that's a 'quadroon'.) - the inclusion of the flimsy adjective 'mere' means it can't be very impressive. ['spiritless coward', Merriam-Webster's Online]

[3] If one were shackled to a young man - and again, this is a completely hypothetical situation - would it be preferable if he were stupid or mad? If stupid you might be able to outwit him, to fool him into removing the shackles once the game was over. But if he's mad? The element of unpredictability would make the whole experience less foreseeable, and possibly quite a bit less comfortable.

[4] So there they were, the young marrieds, allotted a number of servants and a chamber of sorts - miserably heated, set up anew anywhere Empress Elizabeth decided to take up residence. Let us imagine nonetheless that they were given a largish bed, given their status as planned future royals.

noises with his mouth[5] and shout orders to the inanimate armies on the bed, beg Catherine to join him, and hurriedly stash the playthings under the sheets whenever members of the court happened by[6] to check on the odd assortment of noises emanating from behind their chamber door.[7] 'Often I laughed,' Catherine wrote, 'but more often still I was exasperated and even made uncomfortable[8] ... the whole bed being covered and filled with dolls and toys, some of them quite heavy.'"

Thanks to historyhouse.com and Kathryn Harrison in The New York Times, 2011.

---

[5] Can *you* make cannon-firing noises? Clicking with your tongue doesn't come close. Saying 'boom' in the lowest register you are capable of is a cheap yet worthy way to try. Peter probably knew quite a bit more about the actual physicality of cannons (Who lifts the cannonballs to place them in the mouth of the cannon? What is the best tool to ignite the gunpowder?) back in 1745 when they married than we spoiled moderns – so out of touch with the great outdoors and real, intense battlefield experiences.

[6] Members of the court – as hinted in 4) – would stroll up and down the makeshift corridors of the temporary residence, ostensibly to do the young couple's bidding, but more likely in the role of spies sent by the imperious and moody empress (who once had all the women in her court shave their heads and wear wigs ... simply because she could).

[7] Actually, the servants *are* spies. What was on offer was only cannon-firing noises, not moans and groans.

[8] In the early months she still occasionally found his behavior amusing. But as time passed and he made no move to consummate their marriage (ultimately the wife of a lower-grade noble was sicced on him to show him how to do the dirty), Catherine felt she'd had enough!

In which Catherine the Great's Ghost googles herself

by Christine Tolley

Where is "C"? There it is. "C", "A" – What is this? "Can a girl get pregnant during her period?"

Oh, for the love of imperial absolutism, Josh. Your twit of a girlfriend is not pregnant. I know my cries fall on deaf ears. I am a mere ghost, doomed to haunt my pathetic descendants like *you*. Do not force me to visit you in a dream and remind you to court women capable of actual childbirth. Her pathetic, undersized hips will crush the skull of your future heir. Tiny girls averse to cream and meat who run without being chased cannot bear good fruit, my boy. Bad fruit! You could have been a true Romanov had your mother better prioritized her suitors. Now you are nothing but paranoid, bad fruit. Do you know what Elizabeth's descendants are, Josh? Rulers. You know what they aren't? Interns. When I was your age I gave myself smallpox, on purpose, in the snow.

But the last time I spoke to you in a dream you scheduled an emergency appointment with your therapist.

"T", "H", E", "R" "I"— What is a "free" encyclopedia? No such thing as a free indentured servant, I always say. Oh, choose *that* portrait. Of all portraits! Below it: "Predecessor:

Peter III, Successor: Paul I". They should add, "Disappointing Descendant: Josh the Grad Student". I prayed to God that Josh might reinstate and rule a Russian regime, not pursue an MFA in playwriting! The Most Holy Trinity continues to punish me for my insolence ...

Hundreds of years ago, on the verge of my death, an angel of the Lord came to me. He informed me of God's personal invitation to his eternal paradise. And what did my sorry ass do? Deny Him. My golden heart wanted to ensure my descendants could prolong my Golden Age. They failed. Now I idle myself with inane, contemporary amusements. Like Googling myself while Josh watches *30 Rock* and Courtney Instagrams pictures of *her shoes*.

My, my! The free encyclopedia seems rather dedicated to my reign. The smallest sections are longer than my manifesto. "The reign of Peter III and the coup d'état of July 1762". What? How dare someone claim my participation in his death? IF YOUR HUSBAND'S PENIS WERE AS PURELY DECORATIVE AS PETER'S — "Historians find no evidence for Catherine's complicity in the supposed assassination."

Obviously.

Here, an unending diatribe on my various lovers.

ненавистники всегда ненавидят.

Nothing in the agriculture section about draping young beggars in expensive wolverine stoles. I acknowledge it occurred only once, but balancing the ratio of dead wolverines to freezing peasant children was more time-consuming than I anticipated. Ah, a most beloved category: my dramatic writing. Few appreciate my career as a reputable playwright and librettist. I prayed Josh might inherit my genius, but to no avail. Below is the monologue he submitted for his graduate program admission.

ADAM: You don't know what it's like, Lauren. You're an uptown girl. Your Mom is a famous cardiovascular surgeon and your Dad is an important politician. My Mom deals cocaine, Lauren. COCAINE. My Dad left us on Christmas when I was eight. CHRISTMAS. He drove away from the farm in his old red pickup truck and never came home to milk the cows like he promised. LAUREN. That's why we can't be together, and that's why I don't drink milk. Because I'm not just sensitive to dairy, Lauren. I'm sensitive to not being enough for you.

This country's universities might not be so desperate for students if their federal government, say, conquered Canada.

Where is the 'Portrait' button? A pleasing mortal pastime was admiring my own voluminous physique. 'Images'? Yes, here they are. In truth, I am torn between this painting of my face tilted slightly to the left and this other painting of my face tilted slightly to the left. It's like asking a mother to choose her favorite illegitimate child. I believe *this* piece remains my preferred likeness, by Johann Baptist von Lampi the Elder. Strange name, flattering double chins. Wait a minute. Does everyone think I'm a Fabergé egg or a horse? Ooo! A Book of Faces page, dedicated to me. A supporter here penned: "My gurl Catherine, doin a project on u for skool LOVVEEE YOUUU, jkjk ;)." Hmm... ;) must represent an apology for incompetence. My husband could have aided from these symbols. And my son. And Josh's girlfriend. That Tatar tart.

Returning to the free encyclopedia. Altogether, it presents little not previously noted in one biography or other. Josh cannot comprehend why the library plagues him to replace their copy of Robert K. Massie's *Catherine the Great: Portrait of a Woman*. But who can resist posthumously opening a biography of herself by a Pulitzer Prize-winning author to gaze upon especially flattering passages? So many quotations of my eternal kindness. Would this same author recall such virtues if he knew me in the supernatural? Perhaps not. My time as a phantom Empress has calloused me. My genetic perfection has been marred in the form of thieves, psychos, Communists! No fewer than two of my descendants died from falling ice sculptures. *How is that possible?* I speculate my very presence drove some to madness. Josh suspects my existence, but remains too rational to admit it aloud. Remember, he sought therapy the first time I spoke to him in dreams when he was an adolescent. A form of communication I attempt to avoid, yet I cannot help but be helpful. I knew perfectly well he forgot his essay at Cody's house the night before it was due. Was I to let him fail the assignment? No! Should I, Yekaterina Alexeevna, Catherine the Great, Former Empress of all the Russias be labeled "an understandable outlet related to fears of your mother's anger"? No! My silence ends now. This computing machine will grant me a voice. What is that website Courtney constantly prostrates herself on? Twitter?

Catherine II's Ghost @therealcatherinethegreat

@joshr1985 YES I AM HAUNTING YOU WHERE IS CAPS LOCK

Authors

Author Profiles

Claudia Bierschenk (*The Girl Who Loved Horses*) has had poetry published in *Juice Press*, *Full of Crow*, *Public Republic*, *Alittlepoetry*, *Durable Goods*, and *SAND Journal*. Her first poetry chapbook *Perestroika Silence* was published by erbacce Press, Liverpool in spring 2010, and her work has also featured in several poetry anthologies by ForwardPress, Peterborough (UK). Claudia has been previously nominated for the Pushcart Poetry Prize and for Best of the Net. She won 3rd place at the 2011 Berlin Poetry Awards. Claudia lives in Berlin.

Sarah Collie (*Transvestite Balls*) writes in a few different genres depending on her mood and also when and where inspiration strikes. She has lived in Scotland, Australia and now England but is far from done moving around. Sarah is studying part-time with the Open University for a degree in English Literature, she hasn't won any awards for writing yet, but watch this space. Find Sarah on Twitter at @sarahwrites4.

Gay Degani (*The Cossack Ultimatum*) has published online and in print including *The Best of Every Day Fiction* editions and her own collection, *Pomegranate Stories*. She is the founder-editor emeritus of EDF's *Flash Fiction Chronicles*, a staff editor at *Smokelong Quarterly*, and blogs at *Words in*

Place where a list of her work can be found. She's had two stories nominated for Pushcart consideration and won the eleventh Annual Glass Woman Prize for her flash piece, *Something about L.A..*

Mira Desai (*Regent*) lives, writes and translates in Mumbai. She is a member of the Internet Writing Workshop, and you can find her blog at http://www.austereseeker.blogspot.in.

Gill Hoffs (*Crowning Achievement*) lives with her family, Coraline Cat, and an ever-decreasing supply of Nutella in the north of England. Find her on Facebook or as @gillhoffs on Twitter, email her a dirty joke at gillhoffs@hotmail.co.uk, or leave a clean comment at http://gillhoffs.wordpress.com. Her book *Wild: a collection* is out now from *Pure Slush*, and her nonfiction book on the Victorian *Titanic* will be published in January 2014 by Pen & Sword.

Desmond Fox (*The Girl Who Loved Horses*) Ever since a childhood shopping trip, when he walked into a glass door while trying out a pair of shoes, Desmond Fox has remained suspicious of transparency.

Juliet Beckman Hubbell (*Bastard!*) has a Master's degree in English and teaches Humanities and Composition at Arapahoe Community College near Denver, Colorado. She was born and raised in Los Angeles, studied Political Science in Bordeaux, France and has lived in or traveled to over 25 countries. She loves to comment about bastards, humanitarians and language on her website and blog, *Building a Better Babel.*

Kim Conklin Hutchinson (*The Kings and I*) – writer and filmmaker, an AmeriCanadian living on the border – has had fiction, poetry and drama appear in journals such as *The Adirondack Review*, *Bartleby Snopes*, *Prick of the Spindle*, *Pure Slush* online, *Wufniks*, *redlionsquare*, *A-Minor*, *Divine Dirt Quarterly*, and the *52/250 Challenge* quarterlies. Her short story, *Thursday Girls*, was nominated for Best of the Net 2011. A Mid-Career Director with the Canada Council for the Arts, Kim's short films have been in international distribution and played at film festivals in the US and Canada, and she's currently researching a non-fiction book, due out in 2015.

L.S. Johnson (*Baobabs*) lives in northern California. Her work has appeared in *The Molotov Cocktail*, *Cutaway*, *Corvus*, and most recently *Interzone*. She is currently working on a trilogy set in the 18th century. She can be found online at http://www.traversingz.com.

Joyce Juzwik (*Promotion*) has a crime fiction novel, *King's Bishop Takes King's Rook's Pawn*, and a six-part children's fantasy series, *Choices*, published by DiskUs Publishing; a horror short published in the anthology *Deathgrip: The Legacy*; short stories published in the charity anthology *Lost Children*, and in the *Pure Slush* print anthologies *Notausgang: emergency exit*, *obit.* and *gorge*. Her crime fiction / noir stories have appeared in *A Twist of Noir*, *Pulp Metal Magazine*, *Powder Burn Flash*, *Shotgun Honey*, and *Pure Slush* online. She always has a novel and story or two in the works, and she blogs at http://jfjuzwik.blogspot.com/.

Robert Mangeot (*First of a Fine Spectacle*) lives in Nashville, Tennessee with his wife, neurotic Pomeranian and pair of feuding cats. His short fiction appears in various journals, including *Lowestoft Chronicle*, *OneTitle Magazine*, and *Swamp Biscuits and Tea*. His writing has won awards from the Chattanooga Writers Guild, *On The Premises*, and Rocky Mountain Fiction Writers. Find out more about him on his blog, where he writes about everything from travel to Anglophilia to Dashiell Hammett:
http://www.blogbobaloo.robertmangeot.com.

Todd McKie (*A Horse's Tale*) is an artist and writer. His stories have appeared in *PANK*, *Twelve Stories*, *BULL*, *McSweeney's Internet Tendency*, *Pithead Chapel*, and elsewhere. Todd lives in Boston, and you can find more of his work at http://toddmckie.blogspot.com.

Matt Potter (*A Little Squirming*) is an Australian-born writer who keeps a part of his psyche in Berlin. Matt has been published in various places online, and he is, rather amazingly, also the founding editor of *Pure Slush*. Find more of his work at http://mattcpotter.webs.com/.

Stephen V. Ramey (*Catherine's First*) is an American author from New Castle, Pennsylvania. His work has appeared in many places, including *The Doctor TJ Eckleburg Review*, *The Journal of Compressed Creative Arts*, and *A Capella Zoo*.

Glass Animals, his first collection of (very) short fiction is available from *Pure Slush Books*. Find him and more of his work at http://www.stephenvramey.com.

Dusty-Anne Rhodes (*Cannon-Firing Noises*) is an American living in permanent European exile, mostly in Berlin. She originally trained and worked as a classical musician, later moving on to translating, editing and communications consulting. Her first book, *Hard*, was published by *Pure Slush* in April 2013.

Anne Scott (*Favourites*), born in the far south of New Zealand's South Island, began writing in the autumn of her life after a serious illness. She asked herself the question: "What do you do between now and death?" She decided to write. Writing has become her essential companion, bringing life-changing fulfillment and the friendship of other writers. She has published a science fiction novella, *Harvest*, and a collection of short stories, *The Feline Cup*. You can find more about Anne here: http://authorsally.wordpress.com/writers-club/anne-scott/.

Andrew Stancek (*The Making of a King*) was born in Bratislava and saw Russian tanks occupying his homeland. His dreams of circuses and ice cream, flying and lion-taming, miracle and romance have appeared recently in print in *LA Review*, *Windsor Review* and *New Sun Rising: Stories for Japan*. Among the many online publications featuring his work are *Every Day Fiction*, *Gemini Magazine* (Flash Fiction Contest Grand Prize Winner), *fwriction*, *r.kv.r.y. quarterly* literary journal, *Tin House*, *Flash Fiction Chronicles*, *The Linnet's Wings*, *Connotation Press*, *THIS Literary Magazine*, and *Pure Slush*.

Susan Tepper (*Two Grigorys*) is the author of four published books of fiction and poetry. Her current title *From the Umberplatzen* is a novel-in-flash set in Germany. She has received nine Pushcart nominations, and her novel *What May Have Been* (with Gary Percesepe, Cervená Barva Press) was nominated for a Pulitzer Prize in 2010. Tepper is a contributing editor at *Flash Fiction Chronicles* where she talks with authors each month on *UNCOV/rd*. Find her website at http://www.susantepper.com.

Christine Tolley (*In which Catherine the Great's Ghost googles herself*) lives in Tucson, Arizona, USA. She is currently trying to finish her laundry and locate her missing computer charger. She should check the car.

Other books from *Pure Slush*

Visit the Pure Slush Store:
http://pureslush.webs.com/store.htm

obit. Pure Slush Vol. 6
ISBN: 978-1-925101-82-9
Webster Murphy Allen 1925 – 2012. Lawyer, opera-goer, philanthropist, father, grand-father, generous with his time and talents and money ... or was he?

obit. explores the many sides of a man many people *thought* they knew. Each writer has taken an incident or anecdote or memory from Webster's life and created a fully-fleshed man with multiple quirks ... and maybe even multiple secrets. Where does the truth lie? Featuring thirty-two different stories by twenty-two different writers. *Originally published March 2013*

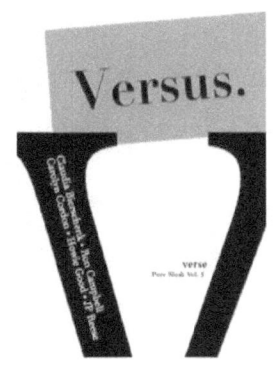

Versus. Pure Slush Vol. 5
ISBN: 978-1-925101-84-3
Can good poetry be written on demand? The answer is "Yes" and *Versus* is the proof.

Bill Yarrow

5 poets write 15 poems each against 15 different topics, so the collection features 75 different opinions. All are different and unique in their own way.

Originally published February 2013

gorge: a novel in stories
Pure Slush Vol. 4

ISBN: 978-1-925101-88-1
Fifty-four stories told by thirty-three writers. Each story is a chapter in the tale of the misplaced Café Gano, a restaurant in a small town on the Maine coast.

The action takes place over one day, and as the afternoon progresses and the evening unfolds, customers' lives unravel and staff decorum snaps to erupt in a crescendo of miscalculated faith and desperate bids for ultimate control. Yeah, it's that crazy!!

For any person who has ever worked in a restaurant, or been a patron, you will laugh aloud at the follies, wonder who will hook up with whom, and at the pace I read this, ask yourself, when will *Pure Slush* bring out the next novel of compilations?   *Robert Vaughan*

Recommended, particularly if you appreciate a bold experiment in narrative and variety of perspective.   *Stephen V. Ramey*
                    Originally published December 2012

real Pure Slush Vol. 3
ISBN: 978-1-925101-90-4
upfront! uptight! up-yours! Cutting edge non-fiction from thirty-one writers who spill their guts on life and love, sex and travel, food and legalities and freedom and family and reflect the true diversity of everyday experience.

Originally published October 2012

Notausgang: emergency exit
Pure Slush Vol. 2

ISBN: 978-1-925101-96-6

Stories desperate and amusing, based on the theme *emergency exit*. (*Notausgang* is German for *emergency exit*.) Scary, creepy, funny, illuminating, sad and life-affirming. Twenty-four stories, fiction and non-fiction.

Every story in this collection, while based on the same theme, is well-crafted, rich in the detail of countless settings, and full of interesting and unique characters, each with their own journey through life, with all its unpredictable twists and turns. All the stories are short ones, yet each contains their characters' lifetimes and then some – each seeking some type of 'emergency exit' in their own way.

Joyce Juzwik

Originally published May 2012

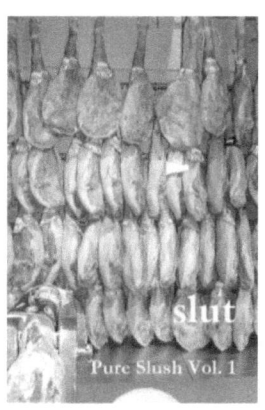

slut Pure Slush Vol. 1

ISBN: 978-1-925101-98-0

a zesty, amusing (and serious) anthology of fiction and non-fiction on the theme 'slut' ... where it all began!!

Originally published February 2012

For the complete range of Pure Slush books and eBooks, visit the Pure Slush Store at http://pureslush.webs.com/store.htm.